BY **Pam Calvert**

ILLUSTRATED BY **Liana Hee**

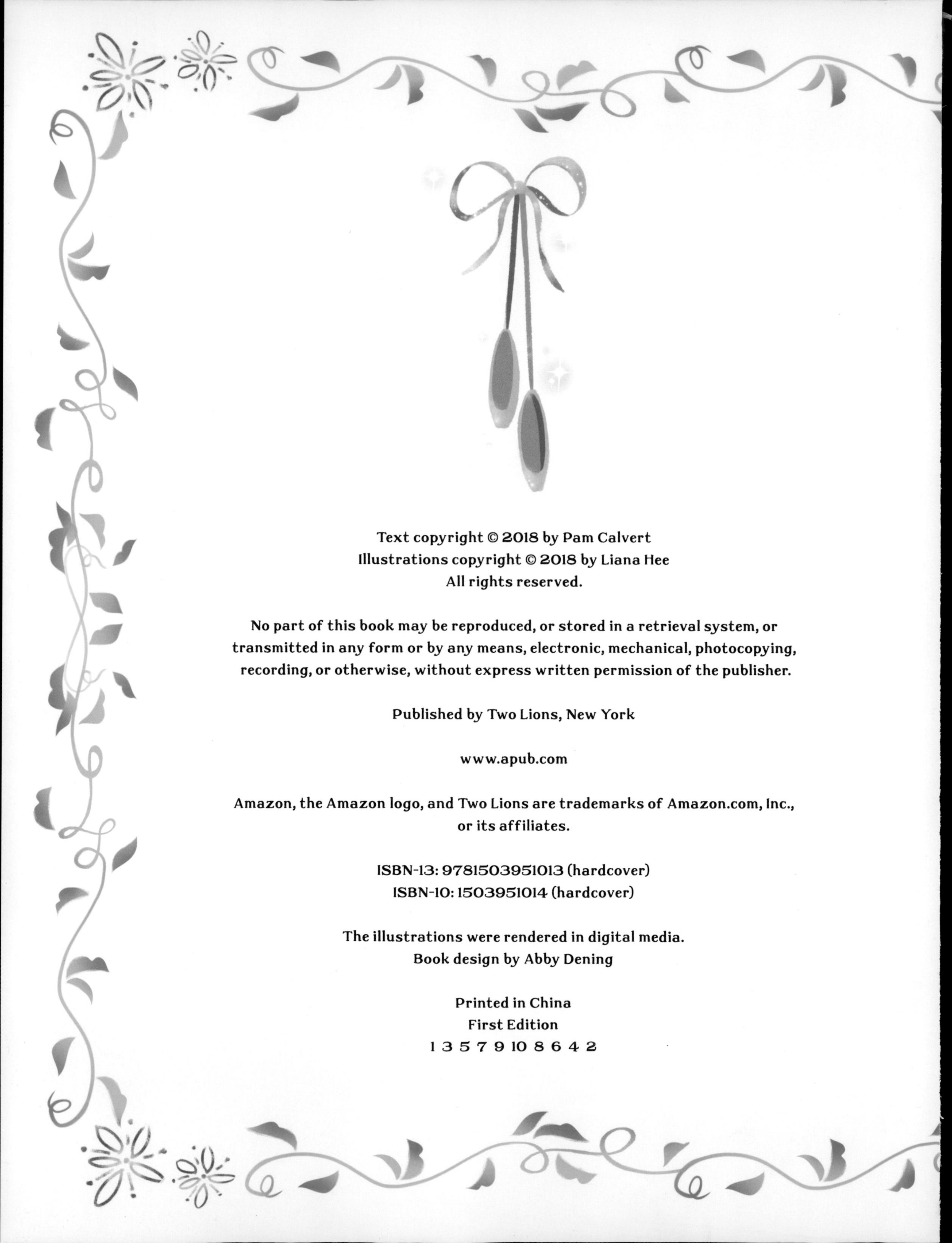

Published by Two Lions, New York

www.apub.com

ISBN-13: 9781503951013 (hardcover)
ISBN-10: 1503951014 (hardcover)

The illustrations were rendered in digital media.
Book design by Abby Dening

Printed in China
First Edition
1 3 5 7 9 10 8 6 4 2

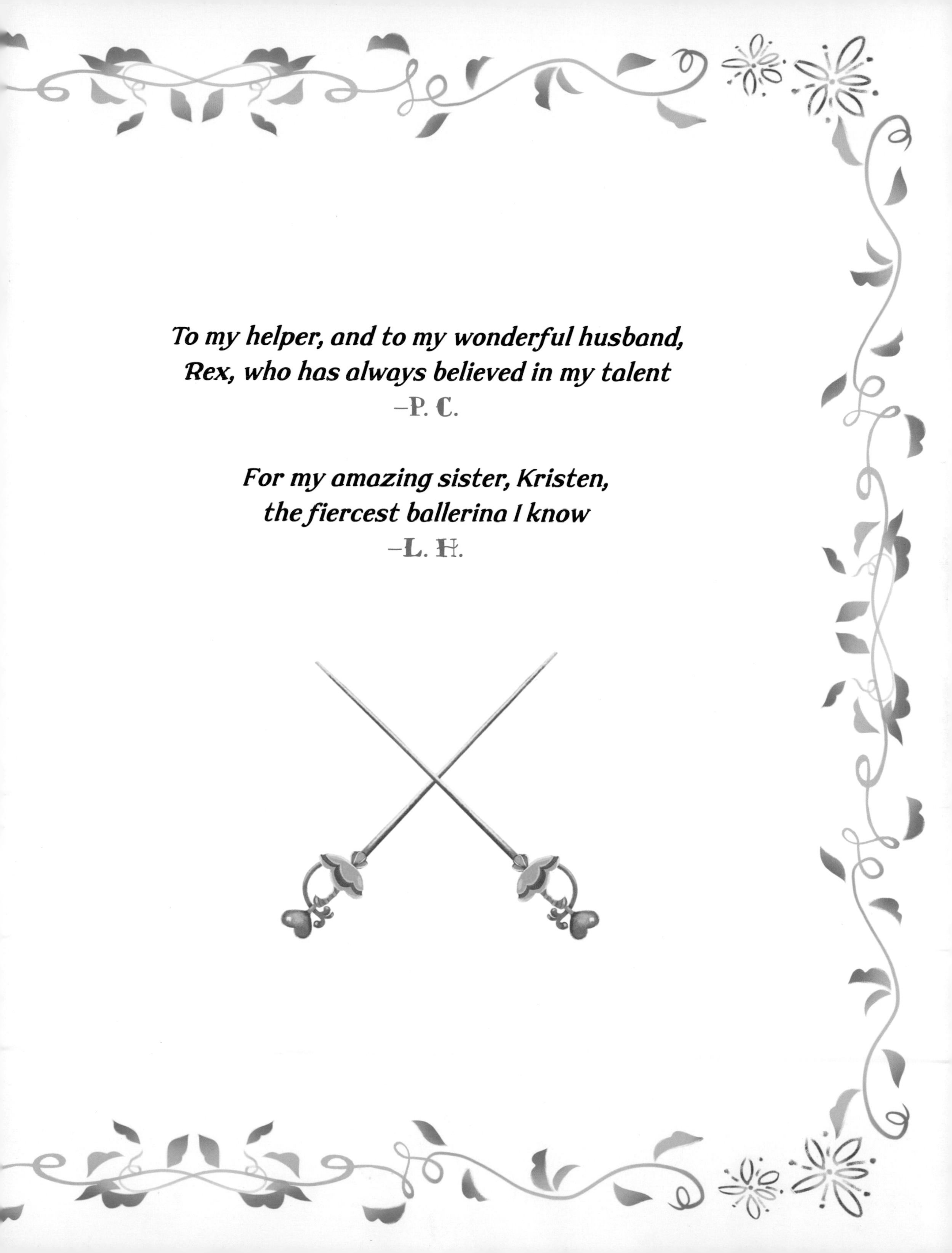

To my helper, and to my wonderful husband,
Rex, who has always believed in my talent
—P. C.

For my amazing sister, Kristen,
the fiercest ballerina I know
—L. H.

Brianna Bright's tiny heart longed to dance.
Unfortunately, her feet didn't follow.

When practicing, she pranced
and piquéd and pivoted . . .

right into the palace pool.

Ploink!

She **plied** onto her pet poodle, Pixie,

and **frapped** into the fountain,
flipping a frog.

One day, Brianna **grand jetéd** all the way up to the throne room, toppling her father's chair.

The king said, "Brianna, my sweet, maybe dancing isn't your talent."

With a sniffle,
the princess took off
her dancing shoes and
slouched to her room.

Pixie whimpered. "You're right, Pixie," the princess said.
"I'll find a new talent!"

During the next week, Brianna looked everywhere for her talent.

She twirled onto the rink to try ice-skating, but it was too **chilly**.

She piled on frosting for cupcake making, but it was too **fluffy**.

On Saturday, Brianna was playing tag with Pixie when she heard a click. And a clack. It reminded her of dancing. "What's that sound?" she asked her mother.

"It's the knights fencing."

Brianna's stomach fluttered.

"Fencing! That's what I can do!"

"Fencing is too pointy," her father said.

"Yes!" the queen agreed.

So Brianna kept searching for her talent.

One afternoon she found a skateboard in the alleyway. Brianna beamed. "I'll do it!"

Careening around the dining room, Brianna couldn't resist peering out the window as she did an arabesque on her board...

Splat!

The cook was not amused.

"Finding a talent is harder than I thought," Brianna told Pixie.

The next day, Brianna found a ball. She grinned. "I'll do it!"

On the royal soccer field, Brianna juggled the ball, then leaped in the air to peek over the fence. She **tumbled** onto her teammates.

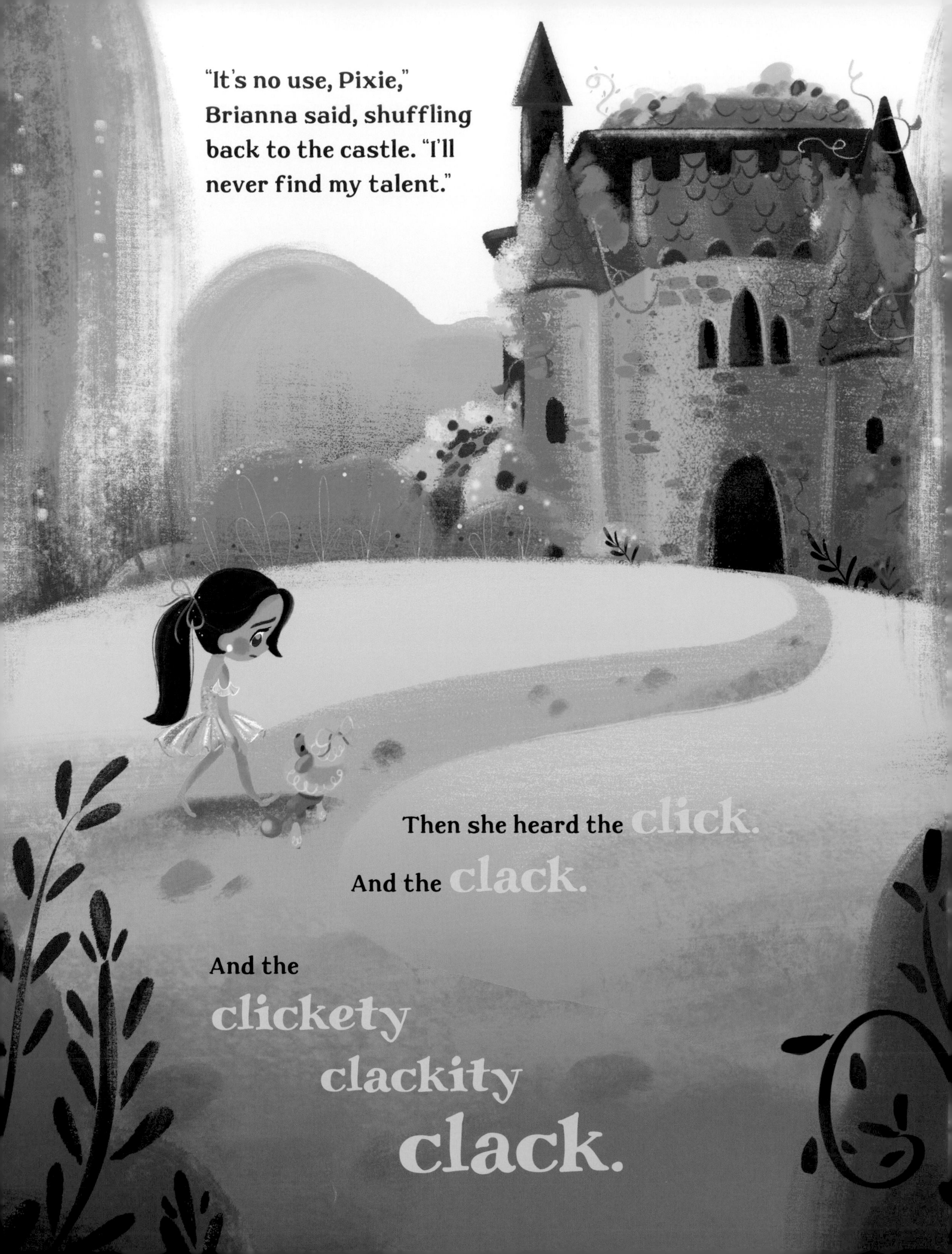

"It's no use, Pixie," Brianna said, shuffling back to the castle. "I'll never find my talent."

Then she heard the click.

And the clack.

And the

clickety

clackity

clack.

Through a peephole in the palace wall,
Brianna spied the knights fencing. Like dancers
with swords, the knights twirled and spun.

"I'll do it," she whispered, her tiny heart swelling
with anticipation.

Noticing a fencing blade nearby, Brianna gripped the handle. It felt good in her hand.

For the rest of the day, she hid and watched as the knights parried and feinted and shouted,

"En garde!"

That night she stole into the forest to practice with her new blade.

It wasn't easy. When she whipped her sword, she

tumbled and stumbled

and bumbled.

And when she lunged, she lost her balance again.

For weeks, Brianna kept practicing, but she always ended up with bumps and lumps.

Sadly, the little princess finally put down her blade.
"I don't have a talent, Pixie," Brianna said, sniffing.

The days passed, and Brianna dreamed only of having a true talent.

Until one night, as Brianna was getting ready for bed,
Pixie suddenly barked.

Pixie howled and yowled and growled!

The princess dashed to the window.

"Thieves!" she cried.

"I must stop them!"

The princess bounded in front of them.

"En garde!"

shouted Brianna Bright.

As the princess had done so many times during ballet practice, Brianna spun.

But this time, she used the fencing blade to help her balance, like a true knight would.

She parried and pirouetted

. . . tiptoed and touched

. . . dodged and dégagéd.

Until finally, she **feinted** and **lunged**, flicking the jewels from the thieves' hands.

When everyone found out that Brianna Bright had saved the palace, they cheered! Hugging their little girl, the king and queen beamed with pride.

The knights put the princess up on their shoulders, and her tiny heart leaped with joy. All at once, Brianna knew she didn't have a talent.

She had **TWO!**

From then on, the princess used her **ballerina balance**

with her **fencing fight**.

Because she was

Brianna Bright, Ballerina Knight.

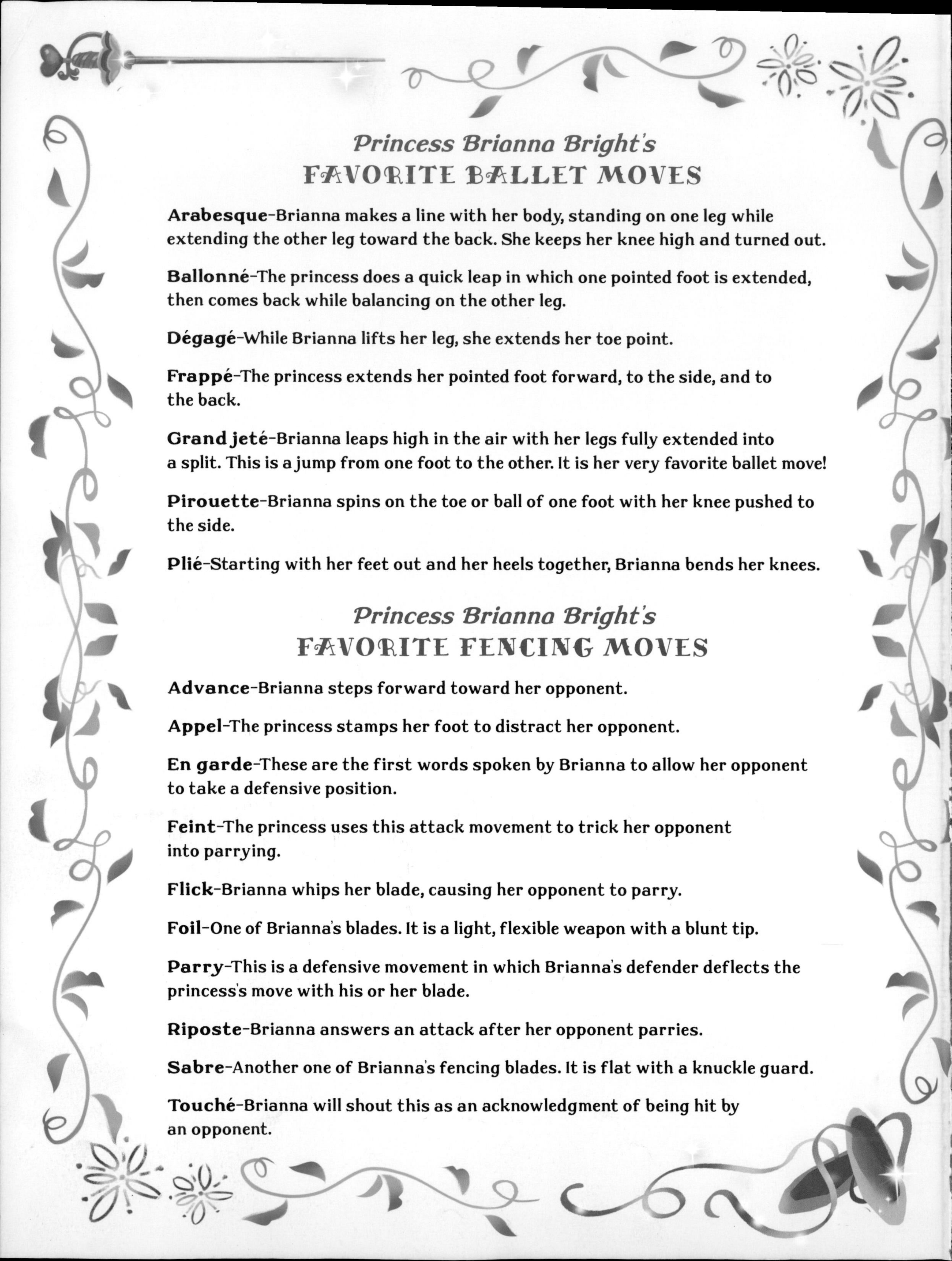

Princess Brianna Bright's
FAVORITE BALLET MOVES

Arabesque–Brianna makes a line with her body, standing on one leg while extending the other leg toward the back. She keeps her knee high and turned out.

Ballonné–The princess does a quick leap in which one pointed foot is extended, then comes back while balancing on the other leg.

Dégagé–While Brianna lifts her leg, she extends her toe point.

Frappé–The princess extends her pointed foot forward, to the side, and to the back.

Grand jeté–Brianna leaps high in the air with her legs fully extended into a split. This is a jump from one foot to the other. It is her very favorite ballet move!

Pirouette–Brianna spins on the toe or ball of one foot with her knee pushed to the side.

Plié–Starting with her feet out and her heels together, Brianna bends her knees.

Princess Brianna Bright's
FAVORITE FENCING MOVES

Advance–Brianna steps forward toward her opponent.

Appel–The princess stamps her foot to distract her opponent.

En garde–These are the first words spoken by Brianna to allow her opponent to take a defensive position.

Feint–The princess uses this attack movement to trick her opponent into parrying.

Flick–Brianna whips her blade, causing her opponent to parry.

Foil–One of Brianna's blades. It is a light, flexible weapon with a blunt tip.

Parry–This is a defensive movement in which Brianna's defender deflects the princess's move with his or her blade.

Riposte–Brianna answers an attack after her opponent parries.

Sabre–Another one of Brianna's fencing blades. It is flat with a knuckle guard.

Touché–Brianna will shout this as an acknowledgment of being hit by an opponent.